In Memory of

JEANETTE BYRD
and
RUBY MORROW
Grandmothers
of
Ian Byrd
by
Jon Greer
David Joyner
Chris Margrave
and
Clay Potter
March 1998

The Shopkeeper's Story

Suddenly One Morning
by Charles R. Swindoll

Typographic collage illustrations, design, and typesetting by Koechel Peterson & Associates, Inc., Minneapolis, Minnesota.

Hardcover: ISBN 0-8499-1356-X

Printed in the United States of America

98 99 00 01 02 03 04 05 06 __ 9 8 7 6 5 4 3 2 1

Suddenly One Morning

The Shopkeeper's Story

CHARLES R. SWINDOLL

WORD PUBLISHING
Nashville • London • Vancouver • Melbourne

COME ON AN

IMAGINARY JOURNEY

WITH ME.

We'll see sights you've never seen.

We'll hear conversations you've never

heard. We'll feel emotions that you

may have never felt before.

Caution:

THIS JOURNEY
may be a

life-changing
experience
for you.

In fact,
you may *never*
be the
same
again.

It's a
journey of
THE
MIND.

It's a journey
of THE
SOUL.

It's an adventure
that emerges

*suddenly one
morning—*

an *incredible*

experience

NOT *to be missed* !

Our ultimate destination

is far... and yet, it's just around

the next bend of your heart.

❧ We can be there

in the blink of an eye . . .

and yet, it takes us back

almost two thousand years.

❧ It's as easy

as the turn of a page.

❦ Well, we're here.

❦ "Where are we?" you ask.

Oh, we're in **Palestine**

during the first century.

The year is about 30 AD,

and the city is

Jerusalem.

I'm a Jewish shopkeeper on the main
street of Jerusalem—Bethphage Avenue—
a serpentine road that winds lazily from
the base of the Mount of Olives through
both the proud and the humble sections
of Jerusalem all the way to the glorious
downtown temple. It's a busy street.
I like that. Being a shop owner, it means
a lot of people come by my place each
day. People from the city. People from
the country. People from small outlying
villages. Having a lot of people in town
means more business, and more business
means more money. That's important
to me.

With all of that bustling human traffic comes a lot of talk. Bethphage Avenue is the nerve center of the scuttlebutt around the city. The milling masses are noisier than ever today, too, because it's the Jewish Passover time in the city. A holiday. That means a lot more people, and a lot more business. *That's good. Very good.*

I've had this business for a long time. In fact, it's been in our family eighty . . . almost ninety years. But I've been in this shop here on Bethphage Avenue only about a dozen years. In fact, when I first got the shop, it was pretty run-down. The roof leaked, the

... it's the Jewish Passover time in the city. A holiday.

shutters were hanging loose on their hinges, the paint was peeled off, and the floor had holes in it. I wanted to have some repairs done, and I tried to find just the right carpenter shop that could do it. The problem was, the best one was up in the hill country, in Nazareth of Galilee—J & J's Carpentry Shop—a father-son establishment. I had heard about it through friends. Had to wait a while, but they were well worth the wait. Those men did an excellent job. Such workmanship. . . such care and attention to detail!

Somebody mentioned that the carpenter's older boy wasn't really

> J & J's Carpentry Shop.... Such workmanship... such care and attention to detail.

> Somebody mentioned that the carpenter's older boy wasn't really the man's son.

NTRY SHOP

The problem was,
    the best one was up in
the hill country, in
    Nazareth of Galilee—

the man's son, but out of pity for the woman who was carrying this child out of wedlock, he slipped away with her, got married, and she later had the baby. Somebody told me that the baby was really born not far away from here, over in Bethlehem. I even had one fella tell me he was born in a common stable because the local inn was too crowded. I don't know the details; I don't get into things like that because it leads to conversations about morality, morality is about religion, and I stay away from that kind of stuff altogether. It's not good for business.

ℐ Oh, sure, I go to the synagogue . . .

> . . . he was born in a common stable because the local inn was too crowded.

every week. And I donate my 10 percent to God like all the rest. After all, I have to keep up appearances for my Jewish clientele. But I'm not fanatical about it like some people. I don't want to attract the Romans' attention. I've learned to just dance on the fringes and practice my religion nonchalantly.

I Hey, I just noticed that a crowd is beginning to gather right outside my shop. Looks like an unusual kind of gathering too. They're not moving along or milling around like the normal crowds do on holidays. They're not window shopping either. This crowd has stopped. They're looking down the street.

I don't want to attract the Romans' attention. I've learned to . . . practice my religion nonchalantly.

They're not window shopping. . . . This crowd has stopped. They're looking down the street.

Waiting. Watching with anticipation.

It's almost like the beginning of a parade.

I'd better check . . . it *is* a parade! Parents

are leading their children by their hands.

It's strange, some of the children are

dragging fronds from palm trees. Dozens

of them. Hundreds of them! They're

waving them back and forth over their

heads. Hold it. Now they're tossing

them out into the street, of all things.

Something really odd is definitely

happening.

I I need to find out what's going on.

I slip off my apron, wipe my hands,

and ask one of the others here in the

shop to take over as I step out into the

. . . it *is* a
parade!
Parents are
leading their
children by
their hands.

. . . children
are dragging
fronds from
palm trees. . . .
They're waving
them back and
forth over
their heads.

clamoring din of people. They're

jostling. Jockeying for a better vantage

point to see. See what? See who?

♪ Stepping outside, I notice the

familiar smells and sounds of the city

as they blend with the excitement of

the crowd. The aroma of freshly baked

bread from the bakery across the

street. And the smell of new leather

from the tannery down the block.

The clackety clack of the milk wagon's

wooden wheels on the cobblestones.

Babies crying. Vendors along the street

hawking their wares to passersby.

♪ "Fish! Fresh fish!"

♪ "Get your melons here! Picked only

They're
jostling.
Jockeying
for a better
vantage point
to see.

See what?
See who?

today! How about you there?"

✒ Clackety clack. Clackety clack.

✒ "The finest purple cloth anywhere! Fit for a king! And for an excellent price."

✒ "Git up there, you lop-eared donkey! You expect me to pull this cart myself? Get on with you now!"

✒ "Goat's milk. Get your fresh goat's milk."

✒ It's all part of the everyday hubbub of life in Jerusalem.

✒ "Hosanna, hosanna, Son of David! Blessed is he who comes in the name of the Lord!"

✒ I know that voice. Since the man's standing near me, I look and discover

It's all part of the everyday hubbub of life in Jerusalem.

"Blessed is he who comes in the name of the Lord."

it's the same one I've often seen in my synagogue, Beth Shalom. He's been a member for years, just like me. What's he talking about? At first I thought it might be a Roman official on a chariot coming by, attracting everyone's attention. They often do that sort of thing, throwing their weight around. White stallions pull their chariots, just reminding us that they're in charge around here, and they don't want us to forget it.

But it's not a chariot down at the end of the street. In fact, it's not even a Roman official . . . or a Jewish elder. Normally there would be a few

What's he talking about?

At first I thought it might be a Roman official . . . attracting everyone's attention.

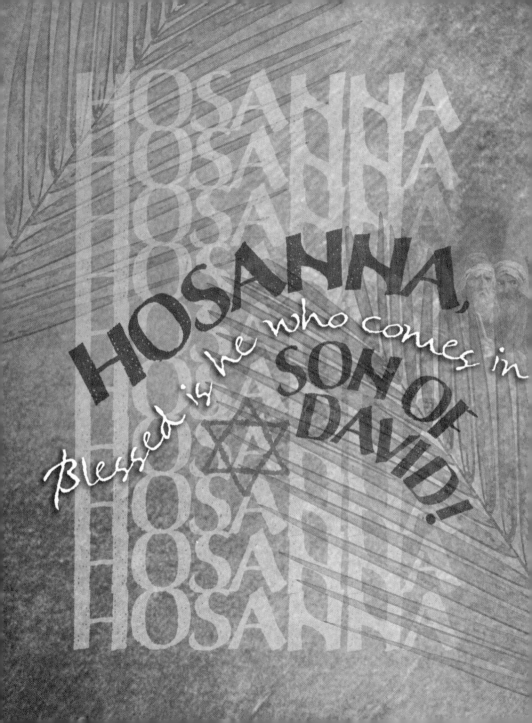

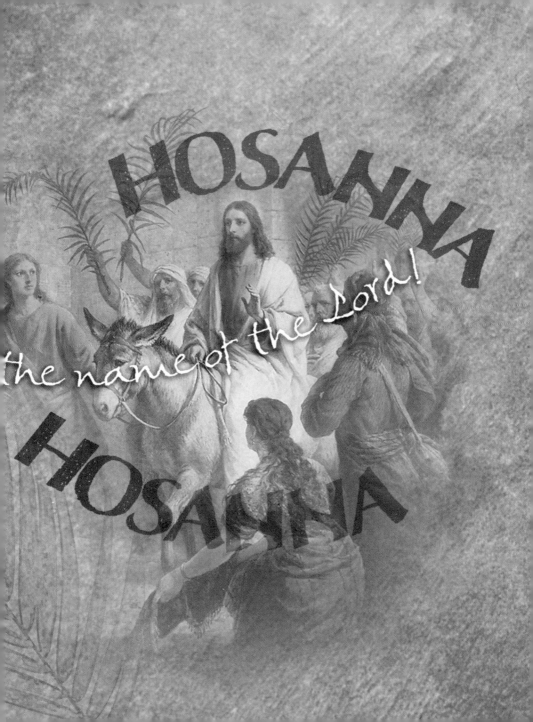

HOSANNA

the name of the Lord!

HOSANNA

Pharisees walking along, praying out loud, in their long robes and tassels, phylacteries strapped on their arms and foreheads, costly prayer shawls draped over their heads, showing off their self-proclaimed spirituality. But even Pharisees don't fit the kind of cry coming from the people today.

❡ It's more of a festive scene. The children are laughing, dancing around, holding hands. Most of the older folks are smiling and shouting back and forth, "Hosanna! Hosanna to the Son of David!" Some people are kneeling, holding their hands up to heaven, praising God. Others are singing the

It's...a festive scene. The children are laughing, dancing around, holding hands.

Some people are kneeling, holding their hands up to heaven.... Others are singing the songs of Zion.

songs of Zion. A few are standing back,
frowning, with their arms folded . . .
curious but questioning. Skeptical.
But most are waving the palm branches.
The way they're acting, you'd think
a king was coming.

I shoulder my way through the
thickening crowd and crane my neck
for a look down the street. It's funny.
All I can see is a young donkey, an
awkward creature with an ordinary-
looking Jewish man sitting on his back.
The animal steps gingerly over those
palm fronds strewn down the street.
It's almost staggering along. I'm getting
a better look at the man on the donkey.

I find myself magnetically captured by his face. I wonder if he's been in my shop before? And so I reach over, tap my synagogue friend on the shoulder and ask, "Who is this?"

✦ "Oh, haven't you heard? That's the Nazarene—you know, the prophet from Nazareth. He used to be a carpenter."

✦ *Could it be the same boy?* I wonder.

✦ Suddenly I realize he's right in front of me. He smiles kindly, and he gives a very gentle wave in my direction. He then nods in recognition. Well, I'm a good businessman, so I wave and smile back. But those eyes! Honestly, I've never seen eyes like that before. The

"Oh, haven't you heard?"

"That's the Nazarene— you know, the prophet from Nazareth. He used to be a carpenter."

closest thing to them was when I met with my tax collector two weeks ago. It's like he's looking right to the back of my cranium. His stare bores a hole into my skull. But these eyes are different than that. Mesmerizing. Piercing. Probing. But full of acceptance and compassion. It's almost as if his nod is saying, "I understand you. I know you." Who is this Nazarene carpenter-turned-prophet on the back of that donkey? And why is he waving at me? What does he see in me? His gaze inflames my very soul!

I I lower my eyes, unable to meet his knowing gaze any longer. I feel exposed

Who is this Nazarene carpenter-turned-prophet on the back of that donkey?

And why is he waving at me? What does he see in me? His gaze inflames my very soul!

somehow. Vulnerable. Unnerved. My heart is thumping in my ears. Why would a simple carpenter's gaze arouse such deep feelings in me?

As the small beast stumbles on, the crowd folds in behind, as people do at the end of a parade. Women and children are reaching out, trying to touch just the hem of his robe.

Suddenly he stops and looks around. "Who touched me?" he asks.

Who touched him! Half the people in town have touched him. But wait. He obviously means someone special, and not just the pressing crowd. I work my way closer to hear what he's saying.

Women and children are reaching out, trying to touch just the hem of his robe.

Suddenly he stops and looks around. "Who touched me?" he asks.

An older woman makes her way to the donkey. "I touched you, Lord," she says.

"I felt the power go out of me," he smiles, placing his hand gently against her cheek.

"Have mercy, Lord," she says, kneeling before him.

"Your faith has made you whole. *Shalom.*"

I heard later that the woman had been sick for many years. But after she touched this man on the donkey, she was never sick like that again. Instantly, she was healed! Just by touching him. What kind of power did he have? How

An older woman makes her way to the donkey. "I touched you, Lord," she says.

"I felt the power go out of me," he smiles, placing his hand gently against her cheek.

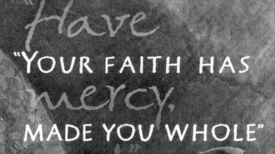

"Have
"YOUR FAITH HAS
mercy,
MADE YOU WHOLE"
Lord

faith &
mercy

could that man on the donkey heal

someone of such a lengthy disease

with only a touch?

⌇ The parade moves on, and before

long most of the people have melted

into the alleys and lanes that lead off

Bethphage Avenue into the innards of

the city. I stand motionless and watch

for a little while longer until the crowd

dissipates. Then I realize I'm standing in

the middle of the busy street . . . alone,

staring wistfully after the disappearing

crowd. Stroking my beard . . .

wondering . . . wondering.

⌇ Standing on tiptoe, I notice that the

little group of people who've been

following him most closely goes all the way with him to the glistening steps of the downtown temple. Now I wonder what he's about to do there? A nearby merchant told me later that as he went into the temple to worship, he became upset when he found the moneychangers cheating people in the temple courtyard. So he drove the robbers and cheats out of the temple with a leather whip. My friend Jacob heard him yelling at them, "You will not turn this house of prayer into a den of thieves!"

What a strange thing. He didn't look like the type to get into a scuffle. Then again, maybe he did, if he thought he

. . . as he went into the temple to worship, he became upset when he found the moneychangers cheating people.

So he drove the robbers and cheats out of the temple with a leather whip.

was standing for right and truth. Strong, but gentle, masculine and rugged, but tender. That was my impression of him. Yes, perhaps he could take on the temple crooks and toss them out. And good for him if he did! It's about time somebody cleaned out that bunch of religious criminals. But I'm not getting involved in that. Bad for business. Best to leave that up to my rabbi.

ℐ Things have been in a constant uproar in Jerusalem lately. There's a running battle between the stubborn Romans and my people.

ℐ Frankly, I've never liked the governor who was sent here to take

ke MY HOUSE

ES! You will not

house a den of thieves!

ke MY HOUSE

ES! You will not

care of the Passover crowd. Pilate is cruel and cowardly at the same time. I can't help but wonder if all *this* has something to do with all *that*. But I stay out of politics too. Not good for business.

    I take one last lingering look down the avenue and stroll slowly back inside the shop. The rest of the day passes, but my stomach keeps churning. I can't get that gentle face and those flashing black eyes out of my mind—the prophet from Nazareth. Who was he really? He has certainly become more than a carpenter. But what?

    Night softly soothes the city to

sleep like a mother's lullaby, and I finally lock up and go home to my family and fireside. A few more days pass, but I can assure you, they're not uneventful. Something's brewing. The crowd that keeps coming into my shop—not only new faces, but some of my long-standing patrons—is whispering and talking more and more about this Nazarene, who seems to have quietly taken the Holy City by storm.

One of my fellow workers, out of the blue, asks me, "Have you heard him preach? I mean, your rabbi is good, but when this man speaks, he hardly raises his voice, but people hang on his every

Something's brewing.

...this Nazarene... seems to have quietly taken the Holy City by storm.

He speaks with incredible authority.

word. He speaks with incredible authority, not like those other dogmatic religious teachers. His words cut through to your heart like a hot knife through butter. They penetrate all the religious facade as he deals with life issues that really matter. While speaking he looks right through you. He even exposes those secrets you've kept hidden down in your soul!"

His words . . . penetrate all the religious facade as he deals with life issues that really matter.

✐ I pause and remember that look from the street a few days back. Mesmerizing. Piercing. Probing. And I find myself wishing I had heard him. I wish he had spoken to me.

✐ A Jewish handmaiden in the house

of a wealthy Roman, who comes into my shop almost daily, adds, "I saw him heal a crippled man yesterday. One minute the man couldn't even stand up, and the next minute he was dancing around and praising God, just because that Nazarene named Jesus told him to. If I hadn't seen it with my own eyes, and heard it with my own ears, I'd have never believed it."

I'm thinking, Jesus—that's the name I remember. He's able to do miracles? Even the priests and Pharisees can't do such things. Who is he? Who is this mysterious man named Jesus?

Another day passes. About mid-morning I come into the shop, and my

"I saw him heal a crippled man yesterday. One minute the man couldn't even stand up, and the next minute he was dancing around and praising God."

He's able to do miracles?

He speaks with **INCREDIBLE AUTHORITY**, not like those other dogmatic religious teachers.

"I SAW HIM HEAL A

They penetrate all the religious facade as HE DEALS WITH LIFE ISSUES that really matter.

CRIPPLED MAN YESTERDAY."

His words CUT THROUGH TO YOUR HEART like a hot knife through butter.

helpers are there working hard as usual. They're a good group. Hard workers. Dependable. I glance up and groan inwardly when I see who's coming—Diotrephes, the Greek who owns the tent shop next door. He's so arrogant. He brags that he has this apprentice back in Tarsus—"such a bright man"—who he's training in the trade of tentmaking. He just keeps talking and talking about him . . . endlessly. But he boasts that *this* is his main shop here in Jerusalem. Boring. Bothersome man. I get so weary of Diotrephes.

Walking in with a swagger, he blurts out, "Well, they got him. They

Boring. Bothersome man. I get so weary of Diotrephes.

Walking in with a swagger, he blurts out, "Well, they got him."

finally got the Galilean. One of his own

turned him in."

✐ "The carpenter?"

✐ "Yep, they got him. I knew it

would happen. You know who turned

him in? A Judean. I knew it. Galileans

are pretty thick, you know. The rest

of his followers are Galilean. But that

Judean saw right through him. He's

one of Simon's sons. His name is

Judas. In fact, it served him right.

He and his bunch were doing weird

things. You're supposed to pray in the

synagogue, right? But he's out there

in the middle of the night with his

followers praying in that park down at

Gethsemane. (Anything can happen down there, you know.)

❧ "So what happens? A mob comes. They have torches, and they're wearing swords. One guy cuts another's ear off. It almost got out of control. But they got him. You know, I used to think that it would be Nathaniel who'd turn him in. You remember Nathaniel?"

❧ "Yeah, I've met Nathaniel. I've sold him a few things before."

❧ "I really thought Nathaniel would be the one that would turn him in. But it was Judas, the one who held their money." I look up curiously. "Oh, now you're interested. Judas handled the money, and he was a Judean."

❦ I wonder what the Nazarene is doing right now? I can't put it together. So I ask, "What are they doing with him? Where is he? Where are they holding him?"

❦ "Well, my source says he's on trial for his life. They say he's been on trial throughout the night. That's not supposed to be kosher, but they did it because they're in a hurry to get him crucified. If they asked me, I'd say, 'Crucify him!' Well, I've got to get back to my shop. See you later."

❦ "Yeah . . . later."

❦ Crucified? It strains my mind. *The*

"They say he's been on trial throughout the night. That's not supposed to be kosher, but . . . they're in a hurry to get him crucified."

'Crucify him!'

word is "murdered." Pure and simple. An inhuman, degrading, morbid taking of another's life. Why would they want to crucify someone so kind and caring? How could anyone do that?

❦ Suddenly I have a mental flashback to when I was seventeen years old, the last time I visited that hill called "place of the skull." I can still remember a couple of convicted men hanging on Roman spikes until they slumped in death. My only thought: *I'll never look at this again.* It was worse than the most gruesome horror story I'd ever heard. I couldn't imagine how one human being could do that to another, no matter what

Why would they want to crucify someone so kind and caring?

the crime. It was indecent. Humiliating.
Wretched. That's why I wondered if they
would really do that to the Nazarene. What

could he have done to deserve that? He
seemed so straightforward. So harmless.

ℐ Lunch time. I reach under the
counter and pull out my hand-painted
"Closed" sign. I surprise my workers
by telling them to take the afternoon off.
Once they leave, I hang the sign on the
door and then, to my own amazement,
I start making my way towards the
center of town.

*ℐ Why am I doing this? I feel as if
some irresistible force is drawing me to
this horror, like a moth drawn to fire.*

I should just turn and go home. I shouldn't get involved in such things. It's bad for business.

Still, I don't turn back. I realize I *can't* turn back. It isn't long before I find myself in the mob of people now flowing along like a rapidly moving river through the city gates and along the city wall outside. I suddenly remember where it is, this hill of horrors, this mount of mourning. There are some profane names for it that are thrown around by the rabble of the city. But I can't bring myself to repeat even one of them.

Plodding along with the growing throng, my mind tries to distract itself

It isn't long before I find myself in the mob of people flowing . . . through the city gates and along the city wall outside.

I suddenly remember where it is, this hill of horrors.

The sky is brilliant blue. Not a cloud to be seen. Sheep are grazing calmly.

from my depressing destination. I begin to notice things around me. It's a day just like so many others. The sky is brilliant blue. Not a cloud to be seen. Sheep are grazing calmly in the green pastures on the hillsides over there near Bethlehem as usual. The spring wild-flowers are starting to bloom, releasing delicate whiffs of floral perfume as I pass them. Farmers are pushing their carts of vegetables and melons into the city to sell. Roman soldiers are riding out on patrol. It's just another ordinary day . . . *or is it?*

It's just another ordinary day . . . *or is it?*

Finally I arrive at the dreaded hill, and I'm careful to keep my distance,

because Golgotha is an eerie place.
Besides, I don't want any of my
customers to see me there. So I yank
my head covering forward to hide my
face. Three rugged crosses stand
silhouetted against the sky.

Three rugged
crosses stand
silhouetted
against
the sky.

⸱⸱ Pushed forward by the morbidly
curious crowd, I find myself getting
closer and closer to the top of the hill.
I try to pull back, but I can't because
the crowd is too thick. Suddenly, sounds
of torture fill the air. I hear one of the
criminals, on the side cross, screaming
out cursings against God, and that's
offensive to me. My stomach turns.

I hear one
of the
criminals,
on the side
cross,
screaming
out cursings.

⸱⸱ Stop! Stop! my mind is shouting.

But I remain silent. I can't speak.

⚜ I notice that the thief on the other side cross says very little. His face is twisted in pain, but it's almost as though he's resigned to die. But there. . .in the middle. . .under a sign that reads "King of the Jews". . .that's him! That's the one who looked at me so kindly. *Oh, no.*

⚜ I can't see his eyes now. His face is so swollen that they're just little slits. I make my way slowly around behind his cross and look at his back. It resembles raw meat, draining with blood, oozing down that stocky piece of rough timber. Again my stomach lurches at the pitiful sight. I can't imagine his agony.

I notice that the thief on the other side cross says very little ... almost as though he's resigned to die.

But there ... in the middle ... under a sign that reads "King of the Jews" ... that's him!

As I come around to the front of the cross again, my heart freezes. Talk about brutality—those are thorns on his head! Somebody has made a crude crown of thorns and jammed it down on his head! The blood has drained down into his eyes. He blinks it away, and for an instant his pain-filled eyes lock with mine. And what do I see for that moment? Hatred? Fear? No! I see compassion. Calm. Pleading. Love! Then the pain mixed with blood forces him to squeeze his eyes shut again.

"*Eloi, eloi, lama sabachthani*?" he moans.

The man next to me doesn't know Aramaic, so he misunderstands Jesus,

I can't imagine his agony.

And what do I see for that moment? Hatred? Fear? No! I see compassion.

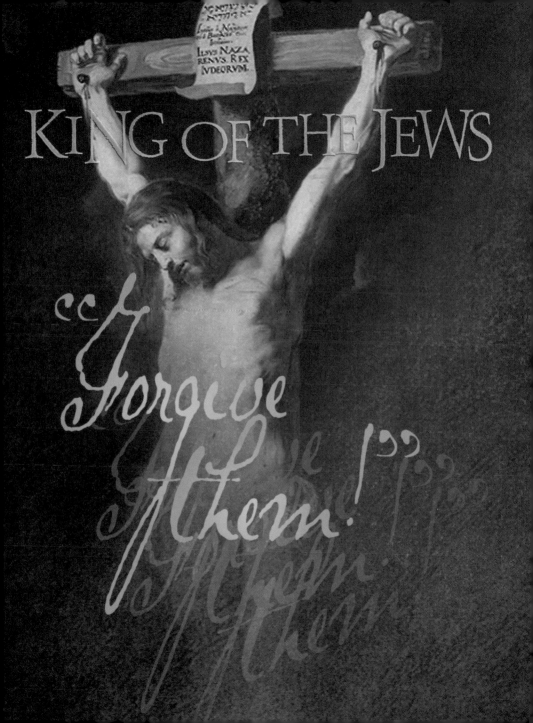

KING OF THE JEWS

"Forgive them!"

thinking he is calling for the prophet Elijah. Not me. I've been in this cosmopolitan trade long enough to pick up most of the languages and dialects spoken in the streets and shops of Jerusalem.

✍ "It isn't Elijah. He's not calling for Elijah," I say quietly. "He's uttering the words of a prayer: 'My God, my God, why have you abandoned me?' Something like that."

✍ *Why does he say that? He must be heartbroken. He feels totally deserted. Alone. It's almost as if he has been forsaken and forgotten.* I remember last Sabbath when the rabbi spoke about all kinds of people who will come and pretend to be the Messiah. *Is this one of those impostors? Is this man pretending?* The rabbi used the scroll of Isaiah to describe what the Messiah would be like. He pictured him as a powerful military king—one who would over-throw the miserable Roman yoke! But this man hasn't done that. So, *could* he be the Messiah? Or, wonder of wonders, could the rabbi possibly be mistaken? I'm really confused now.

ℐ Somebody in the cluster where I'm standing whispers, "Did you hear about the suicide last night?"

ℐ "No."

> The rabbi used the scroll of Isaiah to describe what the Messiah would be like. He pictured him as a powerful military king.

> Somebody . . . whispers, "Did you hear about the suicide last night?"

I "Judas, the one who betrayed Jesus, hanged himself."

I *Why?* I wonder. What's happening? Time was when life in my city was so simple. I sold my goods, ran an honest shop, and aside from putting up with Diotrephes next door, life was pretty simple. No longer! Now here's a simple and kind man on the back of an ordinary donkey, surrounded by everyone saluting him and shouting, "Hail, Son of David!" But now those same people are crying, "Crucify him!" His proclaimed followers aren't following him anymore. And the one who turned him in to the authorities has hanged himself. There's something very wrong here. Some powerful spirits must surely be at work here somehow. What's going on?

✐ Again, through swollen, cracked lips, he speaks: "I am thirsty."

✐ One of the soldiers below the cross, gambling for his garment, stops and looks up. He sticks his spear in a sponge and in a bucket of vinegar and wine and pushes it up to his face, cutting him on the cheek.

✐ *Roman swine! Wasn't he in enough pain already? Get away from him. Just leave him alone.*

✐ Jesus sadly turns his face away,

Some powerful spirits must surely be at work here.

Jesus sadly turns his face away, refusing to drink the pain-killing liquid.

refusing to drink the pain-killing liquid. My heart breaks for him. Without a word, he then turns to spit out some of the blood that has begun to hemorrhage from his mouth.

✑ Taking a breath, he whispers in a raspy voice, "Father, forgive them, for they don't know what they're doing."

✑ I can't believe my ears! I move in a little closer to the cross. What did he say? Could he actually be forgiving the very men who crucified him? Did he call God "Father"? Some say he's the Son of God. If he really is, he *would* call God "Father," wouldn't he? He certainly is no ordinary man. Who

Taking a breath, he whispers in a raspy voice, "Father, forgive them, for they don't know what they are doing."

He certainly is no ordinary man. Who could forgive his own murderers?

could forgive his own murderers?
Who could look into the eyes of his
brutal killers with compassion and
love? What incredible power and
control he has! Wait. He's speaking
again. I take another step closer to the
cross so as not to miss his words.

❧ "It is finished!"

❧ I frown. *What's finished?* I look to
my left, and about four people over
from me is his mother with her hands
on her tear-stained cheeks. Standing
next to her is a friend somebody told
me is John, one of his most faithful
disciples. *How cruel. Hard enough for
a mother to give birth to a child, but to*

**I take
another step
closer to the
cross so as
not to miss
his words.**

**"It is
finished!"**

*What's
finished?*

watch him die at such a young age. He can't be but thirty, thirty-five years old. But she's standing there drowning in grief nonetheless.

❧ His comment, "It is finished," bothers me. I worry over it like a dog worries with a bone. I can't unravel the mystery. Why didn't he simply say, "I am dying"? The last time I heard that particular expression used was by one of those two carpenters who was finishing my shop, back a dozen years ago. Maybe it's a carpenter's term. It's like he's worked to the end of a project, and at the very bottom, when he's checked the last thing off, it's all

Why didn't he simply say, "I am dying"?

The comment, "It is finished," bothers me. . . . Maybe it's a carpenter's term. It's like he's worked to the end of a project . . .

complete. It's done. *It is finished.* And he swipes his hands together and walks away to pick up his pay and go on to the next job. Maybe that's it. It's as if he's saying, "Mission accomplished." But wait a minute . . . *what mission?*

It's as if he's saying, "Mission accomplished."

✍ The sky has gotten dark since I've been standing here. Strangely dark. It's not supposed to be dark at three in the afternoon. What phenomenon is this? Could it have anything to do with him? As he pulls himself up once again to speak, I move even closer to him to listen.

The sky has gotten dark since I've been standing here. Strangely dark.

✍ "Father, into your hands I commit my spirit!"

¶ I notice that blood streams out of his mouth and runs down his neck as he pushes those words out of his throat.

Immediately, he slumps down.

Immediately, he slumps down, tearing the flesh around his wrists and feet. I can't *stand* that sound! It's *awful!* And yet, somehow, I can't bring myself to move away from the cross. His gracious—ness, even in death, holds me to him like wet clay stuck to a potter's wheel.

¶ Someone else is speaking. As I turn my head to see, I discover it's John standing next to Jesus' mother. He's praying a prayer like I've never heard before. It's nothing like the rabbinical prayers I was taught as a child. John

. . . John standing next to Jesus' mother. He's praying a prayer like I've never heard before.

seems to be responding, talking to the same one Jesus addressed earlier.

"Yes, take him home, Father. Take the Prince to his King."

✍ "Yes, take him home, Father. Take the Prince to his King. Take this Son to his Father. Take the Pilgrim back to his homeland. He deserves a rest. Come, ten thousand angels! Come and carry this wounded Troubadour to the cradle of his Father's arms! Farewell, manger's Infant. Farewell, sweet Friend. Bless you, Holy Ambassador. Go on home, Death Slayer. You have conquered our lifelong enemy, Satan. Now, rest well, sweet Soldier. The battle is over. The battle is won. Amen."

"Now, rest well, sweet Soldier. The battle is over. The battle is won."

✍ I stare at John with my mouth open.

I've never heard anything like that. John obviously knows God as I have never known him. He talks to him as a friend. *Does that come from knowing and following this man on the cross? Yes, yes, it must.* At that thought, my heart beats faster with awareness.

John obviously knows God as I have never known him. He talks to him as a friend.

Turning slowly back toward the cross, I look up into the now peaceful face of this amazing man. Man? *No, he can't be just a man. He must be more. So much more. Isn't this whole scene remarkably like the passages in the Book of Isaiah that the rabbi read last week?*

Isn't this whole scene remarkably like the passages in the Book of Isaiah . . . ?

"He was oppressed and afflicted, yet he did not open his mouth; he was

led like a lamb to the slaughter, and
as a sheep before her shearers is
silent, so he did not open his mouth."
A lamb before the slaughter! And what

**A lamb before
the slaughter!**

else was in that passage? Oh yes,
"We all, like sheep, have gone astray,
each of us has turned to his own
way; and the Lord has laid on him
the iniquity of us all. . . . He bore the
sin of many, and made intercession
for the transgressors." *Made intercession
for the transgressors!* He said, "Father,
forgive them. . . ."

I I can restrain myself no longer.
Sinking down to my knees, I raise both
arms up toward the cross and whisper,

"I believe. I believe this man is the promised Messiah. Who else could he be? Who else could have done and said the things he did? Who else could have fulfilled the ancient prophecies the way he does?"

❧ I humbly bow my head and begin to wonder, *How will I ever explain this to my rabbi, to my friends, to my family? He is the Son of David! He is the King! He is the Messiah! I truly believe it! Oh, I wish I had believed it sooner. I wish I had talked to him and known him. Now he's dead! And I'll never see him again. . . . I'll never know him personally.*

❧ Arousing me from my thoughts,

the ground begins to shake. Earthquakes aren't usually felt around here. My first thought is that perhaps it's a large entourage of Roman soldiers passing by in their iron-wheeled chariots with their heavy implements of war. But no. It's really an earthquake in the eerie midday blackness. I look back and see under the veiled, shimmering light of the cloaked sun some of the huge rocks on the hillside breaking. The larger ones are literally splitting apart!

❧ A woman in the frightened crowd screams, "Look at those tombs over there! Some of the stones are rolling away! They're falling flat! It's as if

It's . . . an earthquake in the eerie midday blackness.

A woman in the frightened crowd screams, "Look at those tombs over there!"

73

their corpses are going to come out of the graves!" At that the crowd began scrambling down the hill through the darkness, away from the hill of death and back toward the city. Only a few of us remained at the cross.

I hear later that dozens of people around Jerusalem claimed to have seen and talked to people who had been dead for many years. *Is that possible? Could dead people have actually come back to life?* Then I answer myself, *Yes. If Jesus is, in truth, the Son of the living God, then he can certainly raise people from death.* My heart beats wildly. My mind is whirling with the possibilities. My

"It's as if their corpses are going to come out of the graves!"

Could dead people have actually come back to life?

knees go weak, and I drop down flat on the ground, no longer able to stand. *I* Sometime later I heard that an intriguing thing happened at the downtown temple. That enormous, thick tapestry curtain between the holy and holiest of all, where no citizen will ever be able to go, *ripped* from top to bottom! But that seems impossible—it's a hundred feet high and woven to four inches thick, according to the instructions of God himself. How could it rip at all, much less from top to bottom? They'll never be able to repair it. And strangest of all—they say it happened at the exact moment he died and the sun went black.

That enormous, thick tapestry curtain between the holy and holiest of all . . . *ripped* from top to bottom!

And strangest of all— they say it happened at the exact moment he died.

75

Amazing. Could it be coincidence?
Or. . .divine coordination?

Could it be coincidence? Or . . . divine coordination?

✐ But what really gets my attention
are the words of a hardened soldier
who has been on so many crucifixion
details he can't even remember what
number this one is. He stops and looks
at the stones, sees the tombs open, and
says with tears in his eyes as he looks
up into the swollen face of the carpenter,
bruised, battered, and now dead, "This
was the Son of God." It's like he was
admitting, "We've killed an innocent
man." That does it! I can never erase
those words from my mind again.
I'm trembling with acceptance and

But what really gets my attention are the words of a hardened soldier. . . . "This *was* the Son of God."

mind-stretching awareness. *He really was the Son of God!*

❧ I stumble down the hillside and walk slowly home, each step heavier and more deliberate than the one before. Lost in my thoughts, I'm not even noticing the people hurrying past me on the street. When I finally get home, I slump onto the cot where I usually spend my evenings, and I stare at the ceiling of my little home.

❧ Morning comes slowly. . .but word travels fast. I'm told a group of officials had gathered at Pilate's office. What a drama unfolds! Rap, rap, rap! Pilate opens the door, and in comes a

Morning comes slowly . . . but word travels fast.

I'm told a group of officials had gathered at Pilate's office.

group of Pharisees, a couple of chief priests, and a local rabbi—not mine, but another one nearby. Their faces are grim. Their jaws are set. Their voices are low.

¶ "Sir, we remember that when this Deceiver was on earth, he said, 'After three days I am going to rise again.' Therefore, Governor, now that he's dead and buried, give orders for his grave to be made secure, so that his disciples can't come and steal him away and say to the people, 'He has risen from the dead!' And then things will be worse than they were at first."

¶ Pilate responded with a sneer, "Listen, I never wanted to have anything

Their voices are low.

"Sir, we remember that when this Deceiver was on earth, he said, 'After three days I am going to rise again'."

Pilate responded with a sneer, "Listen, I never wanted to have anything to do with this man."

to do with this man in the first place. My wife had a dream about him and warned me not to get involved. *I* would have let him go. I was hoping that the people would say, 'Let *him* go and crucify Barabbas.' But no, they chose *him*. So, I washed my hands of the whole matter. He's *your* worry now! You Jews have your own guard. You're on your own. Get out of here and make the grave as secure as you know how."

✐ So I'm told they left and went out to his tomb. They've put a seal on the tomb and posted guards to keep away body stealers and troublemakers.

✐ Hours pass slowly, dragging on to

"My wife had a dream about him and warned me not to get involved."

"So, I washed my hands of the whole matter. He's your worry now."

the Sabbath. Nevertheless, I can't get the words, "It is finished" off my mind. His swollen but forgiving face swims through my thoughts over and over again, distracting me, disturbing me. My sleep is nervous. . .restless.

All of a sudden, just before dawn of the first day of the week, I'm jolted awake by a shuttering racket. The hard dirt floor of my little place cracks apart from one wall to the other, and the furniture begins to creak and crawl across the shaking room. Another earthquake. . .an aftershock, no doubt. The first one finally stops, then another begins. Then another. . .and another.

All of a sudden, just before dawn of the first day of the week, I'm jolted awake.

. . .an aftershock, no doubt. The first one finally stops, then another begins. Then another.

What in the world is happening?

❧ My little, raven-haired four-year-old Rachel runs in crying. She crawls into my lap for protection. Afraid of the shaking floor and rattling dishes, she clings tightly to me. In truth, I'm frightened, too. So I find comfort in comforting my precious child.

> In truth, I'm frightened.

❧ Suddenly this morning I find myself reviewing my life and remembering an event that transpired three years ago. It flashes across my mind, uninvited, unwanted, but unavoidable. There was this preacher. Strange fellow. Wore weird clothes. Ate weird food. Preached out in the wilderness. Baptized a lot of

> ...I find myself reviewing my life and remembering an event that transpired three years ago.

His name
was John,
wasn't it?
. . . he once
saw Jesus
coming
toward him
and said to
those he'd
baptized,
"Look! Look
over there!
Behold, the
Lamb of God."

folks, as I recall. John. His name was John, wasn't it? I remember someone's telling me of a time when he once saw Jesus coming toward him and said to those he'd baptized, "Look! Look over there! Behold, the Lamb of God who takes away the sins of the world."

A Lamb! Lamb of God! "He was led like a lamb to the slaughter." This morning it's beginning to dawn on me what that was all about. I've seen numerous lambs offered at the altars. Perfect lambs. Only perfect ones will do. Blood from the lamb's slit throat is held in a saucer. And that blood becomes the sacrificial atonement, that

This morning
it's beginning
to dawn on me
what that was
all about.

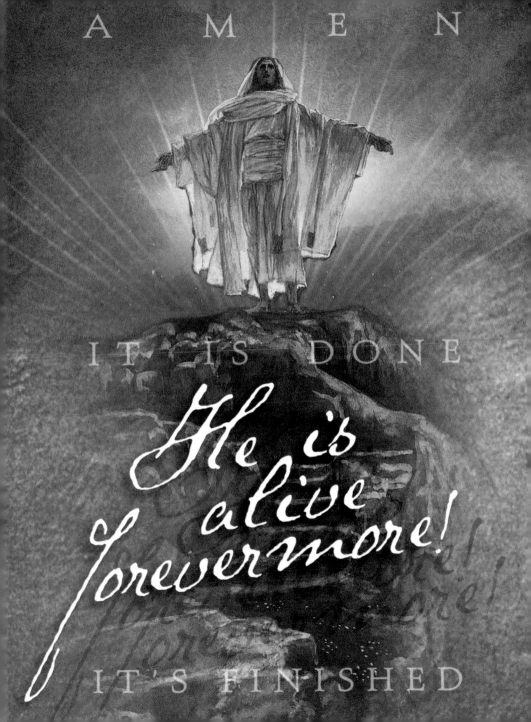

which provides forgiveness from sin.
It's the substitute for the sin of the
penitent. The whole picture suddenly
comes clear to me: *That's it! That's
what it is! Jesus, God's perfect Lamb,
sacrificed on that cross for the sins of the
world—mine.* Now, at last, I get it. He
was the perfect Lamb, God's promised
Messiah, and he paid the penalty for
my sins! Paid it in full.

⏐ I weep with joy.

⏐ The earthquake stops as suddenly
as it had begun. And it all begins to
make sense. It finally falls into place.
This earthquake is like God's answering
"Amen" to Jesus' words from the cross:

**Now, at last,
I get it.
He was the
perfect Lamb.**

**This
earthquake
is like God's
answering
"Amen."**

"It is finished." Mission accomplished. The penalty has been paid. The sacrifice has been made. People will never again have to die for their sins. The Lamb has been slain once for all.

It isn't long before someone in my shop mentions that his body has disappeared from the tomb. I realize it hasn't disappeared. Not really. Jesus has been raised from the dead! God is saying, "Amen. It is done. It's finished. He is alive forevermore!"

Suddenly one spring morning I'm alive—more alive than I've ever been before in my entire life. Tears spill down my cheeks, and I hug my little

It isn't long before someone . . . mentions that his body has disappeared.

Suddenly one spring morning I'm alive— more alive than I've ever been.

Rachel with eternal relief and over—whelming joy. *Alive! He's alive! I can get to know him. I can talk to him. I can thank him for what he's done for me. I can follow him. Really follow him. I can be alive forevermore too! Hallelujah!*

Suddenly one morning my life has been transformed by Jesus, who was once my carpenter but is now my Savior. Oh, what a glorious morning this is!

Suddenly one morning my life has been transformed by Jesus.

Oh, what a glorious morning!

As quickly as our journey began, it now comes to an end. Reality check: Where are we? What day is this? Has anything really changed?

We are home. The time is now. It's a bright and beautiful spring morning. And yes, oh yes, everything has changed! Nothing will ever be the same again. Praise God for his amazing grace and loving kindness.

Christ is risen!

He is risen

INDEED.

Hallelujah!

Praise the God and Father

of our Lord

Jesus Christ.

He has made us his people
by raising

Jesus from
the dead.

He lived and died
in past history.

But he lives
TODAY
and influences present history.

We celebrate
his triumph.
We recognize
his presence.
We applaud
his achievements.
We declare our love for him
in worship and celebration.

Rejoice

then, even in your distress.

He has called us
from darkness
into light.
Glory to the
ANCIENT OF DAYS!
May all creatures
lift their voices
in a symphony of praise.

Worthy, *worthy,*

worthy is the Lamb

THAT WAS SLAIN.

Christ is risen!

He is alive!

And he shall be

raised *from the* dead.

Praise to the risen Son!

Hallelujah!

ℐ ILLUSTRATION CREDITS

Typographic collage illustrations incorporate paintings by these artists. Ciseri Alinari, 46–47; Peter Paul Rubens, 55; James J. Tissot, 85; and Francisco de Zurbaran, 70–71: *Art Resource.*

Eugene Delacroix, 62–63; J. R. Herbert, 14–15; Bernard Plockhorst, 22–23; and James J. Tissot, 30, 34–35, 40–41, 76–77, 85: *SuperStock.*

Herod's Temple, 10; Stanley C. Stein, *International Inductive Study Bible,* courtesy of Precept Ministries.